THE JOURNEY TOWARD ONENESS

The Journey Toward Oneness

by Seren Kersten

Edited and Published by Will Kersten

ISBN: 978-0-578-62972-8
First printing for family and friends 2019
First published 2020

Email:
Will Kersten
will.m.kersten@gmail.com

This is dedicated to my dog, Max,
the best friend I could ever have.
Thank you. Our friendship
inspired me to write this book.
I couldn't have done it without you.

Acknowledgments

I would like to thank my editor, my teacher, and my family, who all supported my writing. Thank you for your support, your love, and your help in writing this book.

Chapter 1: Fern

"Eww! Timber get off of me!" Timber is my dog. A big beautiful husky my mom got for me for my fourth birthday. I'm thirteen now and I'm trying to get Timber to stop licking my face off. He always does this first thing in the morning so we can have an early walk.

"Ok, ok. Let me get your leash and collar," I tell him. So I get up, put some spring clothes on, grab Timber's leash and collar, and we head downstairs for a quick breakfast before we take a walk.

As I go downstairs, the smell of burned oatmeal and liquor drifts from the kitchen to my nose. I groan in disgust. When I reach the kitchen, I see my dad in the dining room looking tired with several liquor bottles scattered around him, all empty. I pour some oatmeal for him anyway, then make some eggs for myself, and take the food into the dining room.

I put the bowl down in front of my dad and say, "Good morning dad." He grunts a response that I don't catch, but I don't care. I sit across from him and eat my eggs in silence. When I finish, I see that my dad hasn't even touched his oatmeal, so I just take it and put it on the kitchen counter. Then I pour some dog food and the remaining scraps of my eggs into a bowl on the ground for Timber. He wolfs it down, and when he finishes, I clip the collar and leash on and walk out the door without any further remark towards my dad.

"I wish dad was the one that died." I say, breaking the silence. Timber stops to listen, but he must've decided to listen while we walk, because a minute later, he keeps walking but with his ears perked up, listening.

"Mom wouldn't be drunk all the time. She would care for me, unlike dad." I stop talking after that, because I know I'd start to cry and that wouldn't be good. Once I start crying, I can't stop for hours.

We turn a corner and I run into a few kids from school. Mean, ugly bullies, to be specific. One of the kids steps forward, a kid named Gabe. Timber growls at Gabe and the jerks burst into laughter. I remain stone-faced.

"That's quite a stupid dog there! Who got it for you? Oh, I forgot, It was your mom wasn't it? Awww, sorry for your stupid loss, loser!" He shouts in my face. I stay calm and then say with a smirk, "He's not as stupid as you. I forgot, who did you inherit that stupid from? Oh yeah, you inherited it from your fat ass!" Gabe's laugh turns into an angry frown and I get ready for the fight.

Chapter 2: Fern

Gabe swings his fist to my gut. But I'm much faster than him and I dodge it and kick him in the groin. He doubles over in pain, but all that my kick did was make him angry, and before I can react, he punches me in the face. I hold a hand to my eye and I already feel the swelling. I ignore the pain and pretend to run left. He lurches that way to punch me, so instead, I run right and punch him in the mouth. He touches his mouth with his finger and I see blood pooling around his tooth, and while he's occupied with his mouth, I kick him in the stomach and then do the grand finale. I let go of Timber—who is barking and growling like crazy at Gabe—and he jumps up, grabs Gabe's sleeve, and pulls down with all of his might onto the concrete sidewalk, bringing Gabe down with him.

Gabe lands hard on his back and gasps for air. I look at his friends and shout at them, "Who else wants to give it a try?" They look from me, to Timber, to Gabe who is still sprawled out on the sidewalk, then they look at each other with horrified expressions on their faces and they turn around and run down the sidewalk screaming. I pump my fists into the air, triumphant. Then I lean down to Timber and say to him, "Good boy!" And he licks my hand. I think that that was a good enough walk for today, so we turn around and start back home. I laugh when Timber jumps up on Gabe's stomach and walks along his body while I walk next to him.

When we get home, I unclip Timber's leash and he walks upstairs to my bed. I walk down the hall to the bathroom. I flip on the switch and almost scream at the reflection in the mirror that looks back at me—a huge, swollen black eye that I can barely see through. I eventually calm down and get some Tylenol and an ice pack to help with the pain. When I finish, I look back at the mirror and the black eye looks a little better than before.

I walk out of the bathroom and upstairs to my bedroom. I walk in and see Timber lying on the bed staring at me and wagging his tail, happy that I finally came in. I sit on the bed next to him and massage his temples. He closes his eyes and his body relaxes.

"We will always love each other. You know that right? Because one thing is for sure. You are mine, I am yours, and we will be together forever and nothing can change that. Always remember that." He opens his eyes and he stares at me calmingly and then he barks as if saying he understands. I smile and crawl under my covers. *A little extra sleep wouldn't hurt.* So I close my eyes, pull the blanket up to my chin, and as soon as my head hits the pillow, I'm fast asleep.

Chapter 3: Timber

When I wake up, I still hear Fern's voice in my head. I get up and lick Fern's face a lot. She wakes up and laughs, and when I stop, she hugs me. I can't really hug with my paws, but I do the best I can. So I put my paws on her shoulders while she hugs me. She laughs again at my attempt of a hug. *Hey don't laugh! I can't hug with these stupid paws. I don't have my elbows in the right place to give you a proper hug.* I try to tell her but she doesn't speak dog. And I understand—dog is a very hard language for humans.

I get up from the bed not really wanting to take a walk. But I do want to go out in the backyard to play. I try to tell her this and she must understand, because after I try to talk to her, she says, "How about we go outside to play."

When she says this, I run through the door, run downstairs, and burst through my doggy door to the backyard.

I breathe deep through my nose and take in the outside scents. I smell the strawberry plant Fern planted (it has a few fresh strawberries on it), I smell a squirrel eating his acorns in a tree, and I smell many other incredible things, one of which includes my toy. My toy is a deflated football from the many times I've chomped down on it, yet we still play with it every chance we get. I take it in my mouth as I hear Fern come through the door.

"You must've really wanted to play!" She says as she nears me. I trot over to her and she wrestles the football from my mouth. Once she has it, I jump up and down waiting for her to throw it. She counts down from three and when she gets to one she throws it high and far. I race to the other side of the yard and jump up, feeling the cold leather between my teeth. I go back to Fern for her to throw it again. And she does. And we keep throwing it and catching it, throwing it and catching it until we can throw and catch no more. We flop down beside each other on the green, dewy grass, exhausted. We just lay there in silence when we hear shouts coming from inside the house.

I stand up instantly, putting my body in front of Fern's. *I will protect you Fern, don't worry.* We walk towards the door, and when we go inside we see dad throw his phone on the

11

ground. He reeks of that sharp, stinging stench that burns my nose. I back away from him, whimpering, but I don't run away. Fern walks towards him and every part of me says to race over there and stop her. But I know that she has the strength to overpower her dad if she really needs to, so I just stay back and watch for now.

Dad says something to Fern that I don't understand at first, but then I hear two words that I recognize. One of them is "lost" and the other is "job." From what I've put together over the past years, I know that "lost" means something goes away and you can't find it. And "job" means working at a smelly building all day and then coming back with green pieces of paper that you can use to get stuff. So I know right away that those two words in the same sentence is not a good thing.

Chapter 4: Timber

The yelling continues for half an hour, and when they finally stop, tears trickle down Fern's face and she storms upstairs. I follow her. I find her on her bed with her face in a pillow, crying. I jump up on the bed and lick the tears away. She looks up and seems relieved to see me, but that does not hide the fact that she is upset.

"H-hi Timber." Her voice breaks and more tears roll down her cheek. I lick them away waiting for her to speak again.

"D-Dad lost his job... and now h-he wants to sell the most valuable things we have. And the first thing he wants to sell is... is th-the r-ring." She starts crying again and I just sit there shocked. Every night, Fern takes out a photo of a woman who was her mom. The photo is of Fern and her mom hugging each other tight under a willow tree. I didn't know Fern's mom for very long but I knew her long enough to know that she was nice and a great mom. After her body went stiff and cold, and her heart came to a dead stop, me and Fern grieved for her every night.

But this is not why Fern is so upset. No, Fern is upset because the last thing her mom gave her was a ring. The ring was beautiful. It has a big, round sapphire in the middle with tiny diamonds all around it, and boy, was that ring special. When Fern's dad saw the ring he wanted to sell it for a high price. But Fern never let her dad even touch it because she knew it was worth a lot of money and he would want to sell it the first chance he got. But what was even more valuable, were its memories. And now that Fern's dad lost his job, he wants to sell the most valuable things we have to pay for things like dues and tax returns and other stuff I don't understand. And the ring is on the top of his list.

I jump down from the bed, walk over to the ring's hiding place, and sit down on it growling. *I will never let anyone but you touch this ring, Fern. I swear.* She smiles and collects some pillows and blankets and walks over to me. She sets up a little bed for us so we can sleep here tonight. I gladly sit in the special bed she created, and my eyes start to droop.

I wake up in the middle of the night and make sure Fern's still here. Yep, still here. Then I see the door handle turn. I start growling, then think better of it and decide to sneak-attack the person. The door opens and I'm about to lunge, when I smell that familiar sharp, stinging stench, and I realize the person is Fern's dad. But the smell is worse tonight, and he looks at me, with a wild, crazy look in his eyes. I growl, and he slips something over my muzzle so I can't growl or bark or make any sound. He clips my leash onto my collar and he pulls. I try to restrain, but the leash chokes me, forcing me to stop and take a breath. While I do that, he pulls me out into the hall. I try to restrain again, but my paws slide on the hardwood floor. When we reach the front door, he opens it and pulls me outside to the car. He shoves me in. I hit my head against the glass to try and break free, but it hurts my skull and makes me dizzy. I try to break free one more time, but the impact is brutal and I slump down onto the car floor, unsure how to get back to Fern.

Chapter 5: Fern

When I wake up, it's not because of Timber licking me. In fact, I don't see Timber anywhere. I just shrug, thinking he went out into the backyard to go to the bathroom. I get dressed and walk downstairs to the back door. I open it, and I step outside, but I don't see Timber anywhere out here. I start to worry a little bit.

Where is Timber? Did dad do something to him? Did Timber run away? No, he would never do that. So dad must've done something to him. I decide to search the house for Timber. *I've already looked in my bedroom and outside, but he could possibly still be here, just somewhere else, hopefully.*

I look in dad's room. Not there. I look in the bathroom. Not there. I look in the pantry. Not there. I look in the dining room. Not there. I look in the kitchen. Not there. I look in the living room. Not there. Finally, I look in the front yard. Not there. But neither is the car, and I haven't seen dad all morning. I fit the pieces together in the puzzle. And as I figure out what happened, I start to panic. But that panic soon turns to anger. *What did dad do with Timber? He will tell me or so help me I will duct-tape him to the wall and force him to tell me, or else I will shoot a bullet through his head with his own gun!* I decide to pack if he does tell me. That way I can survive while getting to Timber.

So I get my huge backpack and pack the stuff I'll need. I pack food that will last me two weeks. I pack a huge bottle of water. I pack a wallet that has around 75 dollars in it, three extra pairs of clothes, matches and a lighter, a box that says First-Aid on it with a bunch of stuff for injuries, a flashlight, the picture of my mom and ring, a pocket knife and a big knife from the kitchen, a hammer and a pack of nails, a sleeping bag for the night, a blanket in case I'm still cold, and if dad tells me where Timber is, I'll pack the gun.

Now I have to do the most treacherous thing and wait. While I wait, I decide to pack some extra bacon for Timber. 1: Because it's his favorite food and he'll come out any time any place for bacon. 2: He's going to want a treat after I find him.

I check the clock, 2:34 and dad gets home from work at 5:00. I make a peanut butter and honey sandwich while I wait. I try to eat as slow as possible to speed up time. And when I finish I'm surprised by how much time went by. Because now it's 3:57. To pass the rest of the time I go upstairs and make my bed and clean my room. But half way through, I hear a key being put into a lock. *Dad!* I race downstairs and once he steps through I punch him in the gut and he slumps onto the floor, holding his stomach. I take the duct-tape and first tape his arms, then his legs, then his chest to the wall. I get angry again. But this anger is different, like I need to kill someone to calm down. But I push the thought away because I know I only kill dad if he doesn't tell me where Timber is.

"Where! Is! Timber!" I shout in his face. He looks at me and then smirks.

"Why should I tell you, huh?" He says back. This time I get even closer and scream in his face, "Because he's my dog! And if you don't tell me, I'll shoot your head with your own gun!" He laughs at this and says back, "Stupid child. I hid that gun well. You'll never find—" I pull the gun out from behind me and he stops in mid sentence, the smile instantly vanishing from his face.

"He's three thousand miles west in Anaconda, Montana in a forest."

Chapter 6: Fern

I sit there. Trying to push away his words, trying to pretend he never said them. *"Three thousand miles west in Anaconda, Montana in a forest."* I open my mouth to speak, but my chin quivers in worry and I stay silent. Then I finally tell myself what I have to do. *Put the gun in your backpack, put the backpack on, and take the train to the closest stop to Anaconda, Montana.* I take the gun that's on the floor and put it in my backpack, I put the backpack on, and go to open the door. Before I go outside my dad says, "Hey! You gotta untape me first!" I smile at that and turn around. I go upstairs and get two things, an atlas that can help me get to Anaconda. And I get my phone for my dad.

I go back downstairs and put the phone in my dad's hand. He tries to call 911 but he fails with all of the duck-tape on him. He frowns at me and I smile, happy that he has a phone to call 911, but he can't use it. Then I turn around and head out the door. I go down the sidewalk to the train station. When I get there, I get the wallet out of my pocket and take some money and give it to the conductor. I go to the far back next to a window, and land there thinking about Timber, hoping he's ok.

I keep thinking about Timber, when a boy about my age or older slides in next to me. He has brown parted hair and curious blue eyes. He holds out a hand to shake my own and he says, "Hi, I'm Jake. Yourself?" I force myself to reach my hand up and shake his and I say, "I'm Fern, nice to meet you." He smiles and I smile, then I put my hand down. He looks at the ceiling and closes his eyes but doesn't go to sleep.

"Where are you going?" He asks politely.

"You probably won't believe me, but I'm going to Anaconda, Montana." And so I tell him the entire story about my drunk dad, him throwing Timber out in Anaconda, and me going to get him back.

"Wow. You know, I believe you. And that strong of a connection with you and your dog will never break in a million years." I smile, grateful for him believing me. And I think of something that might make him laugh, "What happens after a million years?" And as I hoped, he laughs, and I think, *maybe this train ride won't be so bad.*

26

"You never told me where you were going." I say.

"Oh. I'm going to my mom's house. My parents are divorced." He has a frown on his face and I decide to tell him about my mom, "My mom died when I was four. Timber helped me get through it, but me and him still grieve for her every night." He looks at me with sympathy and I smile sadly at him. I feel tears welling up in the back of my eyes and I force them away. It looks like that's also happening with him because he looks down and then wipes his eyes with his sleeve.

The train comes to a stop. Jake looks back at me and says, "Well, this is my stop. I wish you the best of luck with finding Timber, and I hope we meet again."

"And I wish you a great time with your mom. I hope we meet again soon." And we smile at each other and he gets out and walks to the front of the train. I look out the window and continue the train ride with a cloud of sadness hovering over me.

Chapter 7: Timber

I wake up with weird smells filling my nose. Then I jump up remembering what happened last night. I look all around, but any little bits of the house are gone. *Fern! Fern where are you?* I figure that Fern's dad must've taken me far because I don't recognize this forest or anything in it except for the basic plants and animals. Then I smell something different. A she-wolf.

What are you doing here without your humans, dog?

My girl, Fern-her dad threw me out. He hates me, but Fern loves me and I need to get back to her.

What's your name?

Timber. You?

Opal.

Is this your territory, or am I free to live here for a couple days.

I...I don't have a territory. I'm a lone wolf. She seems sad when she says this, so I decide to cheer her up. After all, she seems like I could trust her.

Well, I'm going to make a territory here. You can live with me if you want.

Really?

Yeah, I mean once I leave, you can have this entire territory to yourself.

Thank you so much! And with that, she walks towards me and helps me mark our territory until we have a huge portion of the forest that includes lots of prey, part of a river, and the road which is right next to us so I can set off when I'm ready. She immediately starts digging a den in the ground and I go to our part of the river and lap up some water until my belly is round and full.

When Opal finishes the den, I crawl inside to see. It's simple, but good enough to last me a few days and nights. The inside is about ten feet long and four feet wide with another little room connected to the main entrance for one of us to sleep in. My stomach growls loudly, and I realize how hungry I am.

Opal seems to hear the growl and she goes off to hunt. She comes back with two rabbits in her jaws. She lays one down in front of me and I eat ravenously. She watches me eat and when I finish, she eats. She finishes and walks up to me and licks my cheek, signaling that I'm the alpha. I look at her, inspired by her hunting, and ask, *Could you teach me how to hunt like that?*

Of course. So she heads into the forest and I follow her. We walk silently until we spot a rabbit. Opal crouches down and I mimic her. She stays silent for a minute, then lunges out of nowhere. There is a storm of fur as she chomps down on the rabbit, and then she turns around with it in her jaws. She lays it in front of me and I eat again.

When we spot another rabbit, you try, She says to me.

Chapter 8: Fern

The train stops, and I lurch forward. The conductor calls out, "Anaconda, Montana! Anaconda, Montana!" I slide out of my seat and walk forward. When I step outside, the scene is way different than New York, which is always so crowded you can hardly breathe. Anaconda is all beautiful country and forests and plains. All I want to do is run through the plains, but I need to find Timber, so I take out the atlas and figure out where I am. I still need to walk about seven hundred thirty eight miles, but I'm ok with that, because if I know Timber, he'll be looking for me as well. So I put the atlas back in my backpack and start off.

I walk in the fields taking in the sun and fresh air instead of having some random stranger two feet from your face sharing your breaths. As I walk, I wonder how I'll sleep at night and I come up with a plan. At night, I'll make a fire with the lighter to save the matches for when I really need them. I'll warm up by the fire and then when I feel sleepy I'll put the fire out and roll out my sleeping bag and blanket under a tree to blend in with the dark. And I'll use a piece of clothing and roll it up into a makeshift pillow.

That's a good plan. And I keep on walking, but eventually I feel a great need to run so I can get to Timber faster, so I run. I run and run and run all afternoon. And when the sun sets, I choose a spot with a big pine tree and flat ground to stop and spend the night. I gather up sticks for a fire and when I get back to my little site I lay the sticks down and go collect some rocks to put around the fire. When I get back, I put the rocks in a circle and build a tipi out of the sticks. I gather dry pine needles and put them under the tipi to light.

I get the lighter from my backpack and light a few pine needles on fire and blow gently on them. The heat and smoke rise up to the sticks, and in a few seconds, so do the flames. Soon, I have a good fire going and I go off with the kitchen knife to cut off some branches of smaller trees to use as firewood. When I get back, I put some of the cut-up branches into the fire to make it bigger. I put the rest of the cut-up branches in my backpack to use on other nights.

I sit there, warming up my body when I start to get tired and sleepy. So I stamp out the fire and pour a little water on it, and roll out my sleeping bag and blanket. Once I'm in the sleeping bag I stare up at the sky and see a shooting star zoom by. I close my eyes and wish for something I would never change. *I wish for me to find Timber, and that he'll be ok.*

Chapter 9: Timber

We walk around looking for a rabbit, when I come upon something much bigger. A huge moose. I look at Opal and she looks ready to pounce, but I stop her.

I'm gonna get it. She looks at me like I'm insane, then steps back to let me try. I sneak up so close I could smack it with my paw. I wait for a moment and then lunge out of the grass and sink my teeth into the moose's neck. The moose bellows and tries to run. I latch my claws into its side so I won't fly off, and it stumbles and falls, unmoving. I look the moose in the eye, amazed that I just killed a moose all by myself without so much as practice. Opal comes up behind me and sits down in silence. I wonder why she's not eating, then I remember that I'm the alpha, so I eat first.

I sink my muzzle into the moose's flesh, eating more and more until my belly is taught and round. I walk off signaling that Opal can eat now. When she finishes, there's still about a third of the moose left, so we dig a big hole and bury the rest of the moose inside, then dump the dirt back into the hole.

I can't believe I just killed a full-grown moose! I say after a while.

Yeah. That was incredible.

I couldn't have done it without you. I mean, you didn't help me kill the moose, but you taught me how to attack. So, I guess what I'm trying to say is, thanks for teaching me.

No problem. I was pretty impressed when you got the moose on the first try. Not saying that I'm jealous, but most wolves don't get a moose on the first try. Especially if they do it alone, and they didn't even practice, and they aren't a wolf they're actually a dog. So, great job. I laugh at the second to last sentence.

Well, like I said, I couldn't have done it without you. As I say the last word, I see a shooting star zoom by.

Opal says quietly, *Quick, make a wish.*

So I close my eyes and wish for something that I would never change. *I wish for me to find Fern, and that she'll be ok.* When I finish, I open my eyes and Opal does the same. She must've been making a wish too. I slowly get up and trot to the den that Opal made, and she follows me.

When I reach the entrance, I take in the delicious scent of nighttime. Then I head into the den and curl up at the back. Opal heads into the little room she dug out in the den. But before she goes in, I say, *why don't you come sleep next to me?* She hesitates, then trots over and lays down beside me and we share each other's warmth.

Thanks again for letting me stay with you. She says after a while.

Of course. You were looking for a pack, and I needed to learn how to hunt before I leave, so we were perfect for each other. She leans her head on my shoulder. At first, I feel a little uncomfortable, but then I lean my head on hers, feeling good to have a canine friend, and fall asleep.

Chapter 10: Fern

I wake up and yawn loud and long. I look around and remember what happened yesterday. So I get up, eager to get going again. Right away, I notice two ticks in my leg. I almost scream in panic. Not because I'm scared of ticks, but because I have to get rid of them, and doing that will take a really long time—when I could be running through the landscape to find Timber. But I know that I have to get them out. First I take all of my clothes off and check every square inch of my body for any other ticks. Thankfully, it's only the two on my leg.

I take the lighter out, because I've learned sometimes ticks will get scared of the heat and pop out and go away. I get a flame up and bring it towards one of the ticks. It takes a while, but eventually pops out of my skin and I shake it off into the grass. But the other one doesn't come out from the heat. Next, I take out my pocket knife and flip the blade out to dig the tick out of my skin. I press the blade down at the edge of the tick's body and try to pry it out, but all that does is make the tick try to dig in more. And just when I think this problem can't get any worse, I end up accidentally cutting off the part of the tick that is sticking out, leaving the head buried under my skin. Now I panic even more, and I hope with every single thing I have that this tick does not possess lyme disease. After my moment of panic, I calm down and push the situation out of my mind and focus on getting to Timber. So I get up, roll up the sleeping bag and blanket, put them in my backpack, and press on. While I walk, I wonder how long it'll take for the disease to settle in. I've heard that sometimes it can take up to a month for it to settle in, but I've also heard it can only take a few hours. God, I hope this tick just doesn't have lyme disease at all. I need to get to Timber.

I trek on, and the path I'm taking that was on the atlas starts to head uphill. I start getting really sweaty and my feet hurt badly. I stop to rest by a tree and peel down my socks revealing huge blisters that could pop at any moment. I look away, disgusted, and dig out an extra pair of socks from my backpack and put them on my feet. I also take out my water and a sleeve of crackers. I take three large gulps of water and nibble a little on one of the crackers. When I finish I put the food and water away, slip my backpack onto my shoulders, and keep going. When I finally reach flatter ground, I realize I'm at the top of a hill. I scan the landscape and marvel at its beauty. Then I feel liquid pooling in the bottom of my shoe and I know what happened. *The blisters popped!*

Slowly, I sit down and peel my socks away and see what looks like a small pile of barf. There is pus oozing out of my blisters with specks of blood here and there. I almost throw up at the sight. I eventually gather up the nerves and get the First-Aid kit from my backpack. I look inside the kit. There are band-aids, pain killers, bandages, and a bunch of other stuff for injuries. I dig around for a few seconds until I come up with two big band-aids and some neosporin. First though I pour some water on the blisters and rub away the excess pus and blood, almost barfing while doing it. When I finish cleaning them, I put some neosporin on the band-aids and put one band-aid on one foot, and the other band-aid on the other foot. I pack my stuff up and slowly stand up. My feet feel better and I continue with one thought, *no more stops because of injuries.*

Chapter 11: Timber

When I wake up, Opal's head is still on my shoulder, asleep. I nudge her with my muzzle and she opens her eyes. She gets up and stretches getting ready for the day. I do the same and go outside to the river. When I get there, I take a big gulp of water. Suddenly, I see Opal appear beside me staring into the water.

What are you doing?

Shhh! You'll scare the fish away.

The fish? And as I say the last word, she plunges her head into the water creating a huge splash. When she comes back up, she has a fish wriggling and squirming in her teeth.

She lays down and starts eating while I stare, amazed at the fish. Then I decide to try. I stare at the water, and when a fish swims by, I lash out, but come up with no fish in my mouth.

Opal smiles. *You don't lash out where the fish is, you lash out at where the fish will be by the time you have lashed out. Because once you have lashed out at where the fish is, it would've moved.*

Oh. That makes way more sense now. So I go back to staring at the water. In a few minutes I see a hint of silver and I quickly look at where it'll be in a few seconds. Then I lash out at that spot and this time, I come up with a fish wriggling and squirming in my jaws. I smile happily at Opal and lay down next to her and eat the fish. When I finish, I lick my chops and go back to the water. As another fish comes by, I lash out in front of it and come up with another fish. And I keep doing the routine over and over and over until I'm full of fish. First, catch a fish. Then eat the fish and do it all over again. I lay down and lick my paws that are full of scratches and scars from tiny pebbles and rocks. I look over at Opal as she catches another fish. Then I get an idea.

I stand next to her and pretend that I'm waiting for a fish to come by. Then I splash water into her face with my paw, which messes up her fishing. I laugh so hard. Her body gets drenched, and at first she's really angry. But then she laughs with me and splashes me back. Soon, we're both in the shallow end of the river splashing each other with water. Eventually I get really tired and wet so I get out of the river and flop down in the grass under the sun. Opal flops down next to me and we bathe in sunlight.

Have you ever thought about staying here? Opal asks me. I almost choke at the question and finally force words out.

N-no. Why do you ask?

Just wondering.

Ok...

I was just thinking about how happy I would be if you stayed. Because when you leave I'll be all alone. And it'll be just like being a lone wolf except with territory and clean water and easy prey to catch. But I fully understand what it's like to want and need your kid. I've been through a similar problem before. I stare at her in surprise. Did she have a kid too? But she's a wolf. She couldn't possibly have a kid. Could she?

Chapter 12: Timber

Once, when I was only a little wolf pup, a human boy found me. I was scared. Really scared. But my parents had died, and I was the only pup, so I thought that this was my only choice. He picked me up and took me to his home. When we got there, the boy's parents let him keep me for only a little while. And soon, I became very attached to this boy, who I soon learned was named Jake. He took me on walks every day, he fed me, he gave me water, and every day we played all afternoon.

A few years later, when I was then really big, the parents got concerned that I might turn on them and my wild part would take over. Jake knew that I would never do that, but his parents were not convinced. So the next day, when Jake was at something called middle school, his parents took me in the car and dumped me into the wild. A few weeks later, when all I'd eaten were a rabbit and three mice and a couple gulps of water, a pack found me and took me in. Soon I learned how to hunt, fish, mark my territory, and do all of the things you should know how to do to survive.

But I was still the clumsiest one in the pack and I was the omega. The other wolves decided I just wasn't fit for being in their pack, so they threw me out. I was very sad, but happy too. Because I thought at least I will be able to survive. And then a few months later I found you, and that's how I'm here right now.

I take in every word of Opal's story and I end up feeling really bad for her. I don't say anything though, because I don't feel like there's anything I should say. So I just repeat the story over and over in my head and then come up with a good thing to say: *At least you found me.* She laughs a little and then resumes the silence. But this time, it's a happy silence. Then I shoot upward at a familiar smell. I look at Opal and she looks at me in confusion. I smell every inch of her body and confirm that familiar smell.

What? What do you smell?

Your boy that took you in, Jake. He's acquainted with Fern! I smell her and Jake's scent on you! He was partners with Fern for something called a science fair!

Oh my god! I faintly remember Jake say something like that to his parents! Something like, I'm paired up with Fern for the science fair!

Yes! So maybe, if I find Fern, we can find Jake too! Come with me. We can find our people together. She hesitates, as if unsure whether to go through with this, then she licks my cheek.

Whatever you say, alpha. I smile and my insides feel like they're exploding. I wonder if this is how Opal feels on the inside also. I run in circles chasing my tail on the beautiful Spring grass. Then I flop down next to Opal and she does something that makes my ears turn bright red in embarrassment. She leans over and touches her nose to mine. Then she turns away embarrassed. Then I do something that I half don't think about and half do. I lean over, and

54

this time I'm the one who touches her nose with mine. She looks at me and I look at her and she smiles a pretty she-wolf smile and licks my nose.

I inch closer and snuggle her and rub her nose with mine. And I think that I might be going crazy. But in the end, I know that loving her is one of the best things I could ever do.

Chapter 13: Fern

As I keep walking, I think about Jake. When I met him, I could've sworn he looked familiar, but I decided not to say anything. But now I remember why he looked so familiar. He was my partner for the science fair a few years ago in school! It strikes me that he said something about that and I wasn't listening I was just thinking about Timber. He said something like, "I know why you seem so familiar! You were my partner for the science fair!" And all I did was nod my head, not registering what he was saying. Now I feel a heavy weight of guilt lay on my shoulders, like a tree fell onto my back and started growing because of the guilt it was feeding on. And as the tree grew, the length in my steps shrank.

When I finally realize exactly how slow I'm going, it's already getting dark. I groan and scold myself for not paying attention. So I get out my sleeping bag and blanket and roll them out to make a bed. Then, I collect sticks and take out the chopped-up branches from last night and set them on the ground. Once again, I make a tipi with the sticks and take out the lighter. I touch the flame to some of the smaller sticks that I'm using as kindling and they catch fire right away. I set the lighter back in my backpack and take out my water bottle and take a few gulps.

Then, I realize I've made the biggest mistake I could make. I didn't collect rocks to separate the grass and the fire. But by the time I realize my mistake, the fire from the sticks is already catching on the grass. I pour all of the water from my water bottle onto the fire but there just isn't enough water, and the fire is catching fast. I curse and scold myself for not bringing my phone. By now the fire is rising and coming closer and closer to me. I put my water bottle in my backpack, put my backpack on, and run as fast as possible to the nearest house.

The fire is chasing me and is right on my tail when I see a house. I put an extra boost of energy into my feet and run as fast as possible to the house. When I get there, I pound on the door rapidly and a woman comes to answer. She opens her mouth to ask a question and I interrupt her.

"I need to use your phone now! There is a wildfire nearing your house and if we don't call the fire department soon, all of this and possibly us will be gone! So I need your phone, NOW!" I scream the words and she gives me a look that is a mix of confused and scared as she reaches into her pocket with shaking hands and pulls out her phone. I take it hastily and put in the number to the fire department. My hands shake so hard that I think they might fall off and run away to hide. When the fire department answers I scream into the phone, "There is a wildfire here and is about to burn down this-err I mean my house!" They say urgently back, "What's your address?" I look over to the woman and scream, "What's your address?" She tells it to me so quickly that I almost don't hear it but I manage to catch every word, and I recite what she said into the phone.

"257 Howling Lane, in Anaconda! Hurry!" I hear a pen scribbling on paper, probably whoever was on the phone, writing down the address, and he says, "Alright! We'll be there as soon as possible!" He hangs up and I look at the crying woman, and even though I don't know her, I wrap my arms around her giving whatever comfort I can and wait. For either the fire department, or our deaths.

Chapter 14: Timber

The next day, I feel the strong pull that Opal and I need to go. The pull feels like how you jump up and then gravity pulls you right back down. I look at Opal curled at my side and I nudge her nose with my muzzle. She wakes up and looks at me, tired.

Time to go? She asks.

Time to go. I confirm. I get up and stretch my body, preparing for the long trek home. When I finish stretching, I go to the river and gulp down more and more water until I feel like I'm gonna throw up. Next I go into the forest and stay quiet as I stalk a rabbit. When it finally sits still I lunge and come up with a dead rabbit in my jaws.

I get back to our den, and see Opal at the river catching fish. I head over to her and drop the rabbit. On one of the rocks, there are seven dead fish laying there. I divide the food between us. When I finish, I have the legs and the head of the rabbit and three fish. Opal has the body of the rabbit and four fish. We eat slowly, trying to enjoy our food.

When I go to eat my last fish, I hear a growl from the forest. I instantly shoot up with my ears perking in every which way, straining to hear the growl again. Then I hear another growl, and a body comes out of the shadows. A coyote. Opal stands next to me and growls loudly, giving the coyote a warning. The coyote acts as if he didn't hear it and he barks into the forest. Another coyote comes out. I look into the forest to see if there's another, but I don't see any more. They stride towards us, and we face them, growling warnings and threats.

What are you doing with a dog, Opal? Is he an outcast like you? One of them asks with a smirk. I ask Opal a question. *How do they know your name?* A smile creeps onto her face as she says, *they jumped me in the forest, both of them. And guess what? I won, one wolf versus two coyotes, and I won.* When I hear that, I think we might have a chance at winning. Then I scold myself because I know we will always win. I will get to Fern no matter what I face. I look at their big strong bodies and my smaller swifter body. I think about it in my head and come to a conclusion that Opal and I have the upper hand. Sure the coyotes are stronger and bigger, but they're also slower and less smart than us. I take advantage of my smarts and say, *Is that another coyote over in the forest?* And sure enough, they look around to see if there is a coyote, even though it was a trick. And when their heads turn, I lunge at one of them and land on his back, latching my claws into his fur so I won't fall off.

He barks loudly, angry that he's been tricked. I bare my teeth and swing my head down, sinking my razor-sharp teeth into his neck. He lets out something between a growl and a howl full of pain. I don't lessen my grip because if I do, he will immediately jump onto his back and smush me, but with my teeth in him he doesn't seem to think straight.

Out of the corner of my eye I see the other coyote try to bite Opal's neck. She's quick and dodges, but she isn't quick enough and the coyote gets her leg. She lets out an angry growl. She lunges at the coyote and sinks her teeth into his neck, angry. He lets out a terrified scream and then falls silent. Then I realize that the coyote I was fighting has died. I take out my teeth and look at Opal's leg. I realize something that's not good at all. She can't walk. She can't travel to Fern.

Chapter 15: Fern

The flames get higher and higher until they engulf the first floor. They get so brutal that the woman and I have to retreat upstairs and wait. We finally see the fire department coming and we shout in joy and hope. The flames get even higher when the woman tells me about a trapdoor that leads to the roof, so we can get even higher. I ask her where it is and she dashes off and I follow her.

She stops and points to a trapdoor above us. I open it and take in the fresh air. I put the woman on my shoulders and hoist her up onto the roof and I come after. When I get on top of the roof, it's just in time, because almost the entire inside of the house is in flames. I see two men from the fire truck come out and get the hose. They point the nozzle at the fire and shoot water everywhere. It's just when I see a tiny flame appear right next to my foot and it grows bigger, eating part of the roof and my leg with it.

I scream in panic and pain to the fire department, "Hurry! I'm on fire! Point the hose up here!" The firemen do as I say quickly, and water comes shooting up onto the roof, putting most of the fire out. Then they get it pointed directly at my leg, and water washes over me and I sigh in relief. But it's not over yet, and the flames are rising up to the roof that are so big that the firemen won't be able to put it all out.

I realize the only thing we can do now, is jump. The firemen are already pulling out a giant sheet and are spreading it out in the air hoping they'll catch us. I look over at the woman and she's shaking violently. I go over and put my arms on her.

"What's wrong?" I scream over the crackling fire. Her voice trembles, and I have to lean in to hear her speak.

"I-I'm afr-fraid of heights!" I look from her, to down below, to her and down below, and I say, "we'll jump together on the count of three." She looks at me and nods slowly, afraid.

"One, two, three!" I wrap my arms around her and jump. She screams while we fall into the sheet, but we make it. I get out of the sheet quickly and so does the woman. I watch the house burn from afar and I groan in pain as I slowly take off one of my shoes and then peel off one of my socks. What I see is a burn all over my foot that is a deep red and shiny and bloody and raw. I groan again as I remember my First-Aid kit in my backpack. I reach over to my backpack that somehow survived the fire, and I pull out my First-Aid kit.

I move my hand all around in there until I find some cream that soothes and helps heal first degree to third degree burns and I'd say mine is about a third. I dip my fingers in the cream and pull them out and spread the cream all over my foot. I bite my lip so hard that I taste blood to muffle a scream from the pain, but then that pain suddenly just goes away like it was never there.

I sigh in relief and happiness. I look at the label on the cream and it says, *Spread the cream over your burn every morning and night, and in about three days, it will heal completely.* I almost scream out loud but I manage to control it. I try to push away what I read but every time I try I just stare at it more. *Three days! That will take forever! I need to find Timber now or else I may never will. No, I will keep going while it's healing. But first, I need crutches and more water.*

Chapter 16: Fern

I put the cream back in the kit, and the kit back in my backpack. I look around and see a tree with low branches. I manage to get up and limp over to the tree. I take out the kitchen knife from my backpack and saw off two branches. They fall to the ground with a thud and I line them up next to each other. They are sturdy, reliable, and strong. I pick up one of the branches and see how long I will need it to be in order to easily fit my arm over them. When I finish, I lay the one I was using back on the ground and saw some of the end off. I do the same to the other one until they are the perfect height for me and the same height as each other.

I test them under my armpits and I remember I need to add some padding for that part. I think of what I could use as padding and remember I have extra clothes. I take out a fuzzy hoodie from my backpack and use the scissors from the First-Aid kit to cut off the ends of the sleeves. I trim the ends until they are fit for crutches. Next, I go around and look for two smaller sticks and find some laying in a heap on the ground. I pick them up and carry them back to the make-shift crutches.

I take out the hammer and nails and pound one of the sticks on an end of one of the branches, and do the same to the others. I take out the ends of the sleeves and hammer some nails through the sleeves and into the sticks.

So now, each crutch looks like this: a branch with a stick on one of the ends so it looks like a big letter T, with the end of a sleeve rolled around the small stick on top that's nailed through. I carefully put them under my armpits again, and this time, with the sleeves on top, the crutches are comfortable, strong, sturdy, reliable, and soft. I carefully try walking around with them. I plant the crutches in front of me, and take a swing. I land in front of the crutches on the ground smoothly, like I've done this my whole life. I take a few more practice-swings until I'm sure that they'll work out.

I pick up my backpack and heave it onto my shoulders. It's a little harder to swing with my backpack on, but I still do ok. Now I start looking for a source of water. I now fully regret dumping the water out of my water bottle onto the fire, since it didn't do anything to stop it. I suddenly realize that with all that's been going on, I've forgotten about Timber. A big pit grows in my stomach as I think of what could be happening to him and I haven't thought about him at all. I try to focus on finding water but my thoughts keep sending me back to Timber as I realize I can look for him and look for water at the same time. I get the atlas out of my backpack, flip to the United States, and find Anaconda, Montana. I breathe a huge sigh of relief as I notice that I'm not too far off track. I put the book away and head in the direction of Timber.

Once I'm back on track, I start getting really thirsty. I keep walking for three hours, and still no water. My vision gets hazy and my throat feels like sandpaper, scratchy and dry. I keep going and I can feel my body shutting down when I see it. A lake full of water. I go as fast as I can with my crutches towards the lake and I stop shortly to catch my breath. I'm parched and exhausted and I can barely keep my eyes open. I head towards the water still, but half-way there, I stumble and fall, and I don't get up for a long time.

Chapter 17: Timber

I practically drag Opal to the shallow end of the river, careful of not hurting her leg. I pull her body into the water and splash water onto her wound. She yelps in pain a few times. Once we're done in the river, I heave her onto the freshly grown, sweet smelling grass. I lay next to her and start licking the blood away, cleaning the wound. I know that she won't heal for a while, but she says she's strong enough to keep traveling to Fern.

When I finish cleaning the wound, blood doesn't spill out anymore, and all you see are teeth marks in her leg. I help her up and she limps around, strengthening her leg which she'll be walking on for quite a while. Every time she stumbles, I race over to her and help her up. Soon, she's limping but she's strong.

Get some rest in the den. I'm going to hunt. I say to her after a while of limping, strengthening, and training her on one leg. She looks at me and nods.

Be careful Timber.

You too, Opal. And she turns around and heads back to the den while I stalk into the forest quietly and carefully. I look around and spot a deer. I go through the hunting methods in my head that Opal taught me, and once I'm all caught up, I start creeping over. I get so close that I can almost touch it, but the deer must've heard me and she puts on a burst of speed and dashes away. I'm too tired from training Opal to follow the deer, so I just keep stalking the forest.

I keep going for an hour when Opal howls to make sure I'm ok. I howl back, telling her I'm fine, just having hunting trouble. Then I remember something. I howl to say that I have an idea and I'm coming back. And before she can respond, I'm dashing towards her scent. When I'm at the edge of the forest I go over to a tree that I marked, and I start digging in the dirt. I begin to see a carcass in the dirt. I bark to Opal excitedly.

Remember my first kill? The moose! But we couldn't finish it so we buried it here for later. And now we really need it!

Of course! All that time hunting, we could've been digging for the moose! Timber you're so smart! She bumps my nose with hers real quick then turns away embarrassed when I lean over and lick her nose and bump it back with my own. She looks at me, happy, then digs next to me and helps pull the carcass out of the hole. We drag it to the den and start eating. We eat the entire carcass, and with our bellies full, we go outside and start playing tag. We keep running and limping until we're super tired. She winces a little bit when she lays down, but other than that, she doesn't show any sign of her leg hurting.

I snuggle next to her and lick her nose. She licks back happily. I get even closer and snuggle her more, making sure she's safe. Eventually my eyes droop and I drift off in happy dreams of me and Fern reunited.

Chapter 18: Timber

When I wake up, there's that feeling in the air again, that pull, that tells me we should get going. I nudge Opal gently, telling her it's time to go. She seems eager to get going and so am I. I get up and stretch all of my muscles and help Opal walk out of the den. She lays down on the grass outside. I go into the forest and come back with a deer in my mouth. I lay it down in front of Opal and we both start eating. We eat all of it in case we don't encounter food for the next few days. Opal and I get up and go to the river. We gulp down water and then I clean Opal's wound again, making sure to get it nice and clean.

I stand up boldly and sniff the air for the road. I go in the direction of where the road is, and when I get there, Opal is right next to me. She stands boldly with a kind of ferocity that almost scares me. She doesn't even seem to notice her damaged leg as she limps around. I sniff the air again hoping that Fern's car's scent would still be there. At first, I smell nothing and I start to panic, but then the wind changes direction and blows Fern's car's scent right into my face, and all of my panic turns into happiness. I sniff the air one last time and then drop my head to the side of the road, following the car's scent. Opal follows behind me and looks around anxiously. I whimper to her and comfort her that I would never let a car get us.

We keep going for hours and hours. While we track the car's scent, Opal tells me about Jake, how nice and kind he is, and how playful he is. Then she asks about what Fern is like, and I give her a full-blown description. Opal utters some words of relief under her breath as she hears how amazing Fern is. Then I stop dead in my tracks and ask Opal something that just popped into my mind that I would really like to happen.

Opal.

Yes Timber?

Have you ever thought of...of what would happen if Fern and Jake lived together? I mean, if they did, we would be able to have puppies and never be apart, and Fern and Jake are really good friends. And Fern would never want to live with her father ever again. Then again, you said Jake's parents are never together anymore, so I don't know how that would work out. She looks at me and nods mostly to herself. I keep walking and we don't start a conversation anymore. And I can tell that we both have the same thing on our minds. *Would it work out?* I tumble the question over and over in my head and never come to a conclusion. I eventually push the thought away and focus instead on about how happy Fern would be to see me again. I'll see her and she'll see me at the exact same moment, and we'll run into each other's arms and paws and hug, never letting go.

Then I hear a sound and come back to my senses. I see headlights coming from up ahead and bark to Opal to stand back because there's a car coming. She jumps back immediately and I stand back with her as the car goes by. And the question again pops into my head. *Would it somehow work out?*

Chapter 19: Fern

Finally I wake and remember what happened. I scold myself, knowing that I can't afford to pass out again or I might never wake up. My throat is dry and hoarse and when I try to speak I feel like I'm trying to swallow knives. Then I remember that I'm near a lake. I try to get up but my body is as stiff as cardboard and won't allow myself to get up. Eventually I calm down and slowly place my hands and knees on the ground and start to crawl towards the lake.

When I get there, I brace myself to plunge into the water. I close my eyes and collapse into the water. I swim to shallower water and drink and drink and drink. I drink and swim for what seems like hours and when I finish I feel like a whole new person. I get up slowly and limp back towards my backpack and crutches. I slide the crutches underneath my arms and carry my backpack over to the water.

I take out my water bottle and fill it with lake water all the way to the top and drink it all down. I keep refilling my water bottle, then drinking it down. When I've had enough water, I fill up my water bottle to the top and put it back in my backpack. I just sit there and splash my face with water trying to get the dirt off when I have a better idea.

I look around to make sure no one is here and I slowly peel off my soaked clothes and lay them on the grass to dry. I take out the change of clothes from my backpack and lay them down for when I'm done. Completely naked, I jump into the lake and let the cold water wash over me. Even though I have no soap, I clean off what dirt and mud I can, careful when cleaning the dirt from my feet.

When I get out, I shake like a wet dog and use one of my hoodies to dry off. When I do, I take my new clothes and put them on. A T-shirt, sweatpants, fuzzy socks, a hoodie, and underwear. Once I'm all clothed up, I slip one hiking boot onto my right foot and lace it up tight. Then I slowly and carefully slip my other hiking boot onto my left foot and lace it looser than the other one, careful of the burn from the fire. I take out an apple and four crackers and cheese and eat a small, but satisfying, picnic.

I eat slowly, savoring every bite, and when I'm done, I put my backpack on my back and get back onto the path towards where Dad left Timber. I start singing randomly a few hours later while I swing on my crutches. The song is one my mother sang every day and tears well up in my eyes whenever I think of it. I sing and swing until it gets dark and I slap myself in the face for remembering how stupidly I forgot the rocks last night and started a wildfire.

The first thing I do is collect rocks for the fire ring so I don't forget like I did last night. Then I get the last chopped-up branches from my backpack and gather some small sticks. Again, I put the sticks in a tipi formation and pull out the lighter. I light the sticks on fire and put a piece of chopped-up branch on top. Once the fire is going well, I decide to chop up another branch for tomorrow night. I get out the kitchen knife and saw off a branch and bring it over to the fire so I don't lose sight of it and it gets out of control. I saw off chunks of the branch and roll them into my backpack. Once I finish, I get out my sleeping gear and make a bed for the night. I stamp out the fire and stare at the stars. I close my eyes and fall asleep with a single thought in my head. *I will find you Timber. You can count on it.*

Chapter 20: Timber

We keep going until the sun sets. I bark to Opal when I find a good spot to spend the night. I head into the forest and curl up inside a little burrow under a fallen tree. Opal joins me and sleepily snuggles into my fur. My eyes droop and I say goodnight, and before I hear her response, I'm fast asleep.

"T-Timb-b-b-ber. C-Come h-h-here." I look around and see Fern with her arms outstretched wide and I start running towards her but recoil just before I reach her. Her pupils are blood red and her skin reeks of that sharp stinging stench that her dad smells of. I fold my ears back and tuck my tail under my legs and whine softly, afraid of what she has become.

H-Hell-ll-llo T-Timberr. C-Come p-p-play with m-me! I see Opal creep out from behind Fern and her pupils are blood red too. She reeks of blood and flesh. I look from one to the other, scared out of my skull. Suddenly, Opal growls and lunges at me. She pins me down with her paws and I try to squirm away, but her massive strength compared to my slim, skinny body gives her the upper hand. Fern walks to us, hoists me into her arms, and crosses over to a tree without speaking. I struggle to jump or twist out of her arms, but she holds me with greater strength. She brings out ropes, and with one hand, holds me against the tree, and with the other hand, starts wrapping the rope around me, then slips her hand away and ties me up tighter.

She pulls the rope with tremendous strength and I almost choke. Opal circles the tree below me, growling, then stalks away behind Fern. Fern gathers up sticks and makes a tipi formation under me and takes out a lighter. I bark and growl and whimper in terror. Fern brings the lighter to the sticks. A flame appears out of the lighter and catches on the sticks. I howl, scared, confused, and angry. The flames rise higher and burn my paws, and I yelp and howl in pain as the flames rise even higher.

And just before the flames engulf my entire body, Fern says something that hurts me more than any flame could.

"Dad was right to throw you away. I now realize that. Somehow you survived when you weren't supposed to, so now, I'm helping my dad finish the job." She smiles wickedly and the last I hear and see is Opal being picked up into Fern's arms and Fern saying, "Good job Opal. You're better than any Timber." She smiles another wicked smile, then the flames take away my vision, and my life.

Chapter 21: Fern

I wake up with a confidence and energy that gets me to my feet right away because today I'm determined to get at least a quarter way to Timber. I unpack a few things, take a couple gulps of water, an apple and carrots, and then pack it all back up including my sleeping gear. I heave my backpack onto my shoulders and pick up my crutches. I start walking towards Timber right away—excited, even though I've no idea why. It's slow-going on my crutches. After a few hours, I take a break for water and pull out the atlas.

I trace my finger from my home, to where I am now, to where dad kicked Timber out. I do the math in my head and decide that I still have about three hundred eighty five miles left to go. I get really excited because I have only been traveling to Timber for about four to five days and I thought by now I would've been traveling for seven to eight. I put the atlas back and resume walking again.

I go for a couple of hours when I shriek as a shot of pain shoots through my back. The pain only lasts a second and doesn't hurt too bad afterwards. But as I keep swinging I notice aches and pains creep through my body. At one point I stop because of a cramp in my stomach. Retracing my journey, I wonder what could've caused these aches and pains, and at first, I come up with nothing.

Then I remember, I never actually got that second tick out and it's still in my body. I stop for a moment as my eyes sneak a glance downward at my pant leg where the tick is. I breathe deeply and know I have to check. So I move my hand to the bottom of my pant leg, grab it firmly in my hands, and yank up, fearing what I might see. When I see no maroon ring around the wound—the tell-tale sign of lyme disease—I let out a deep breath that I didn't know I was holding in. I decide the aches and pains are just from walking so much, so I let go of my pant leg and keep going.

I hobble along all day, ignoring the pain in my body. When night comes, I know that I've lost enough time already so I take out my flashlight, turn it on, and keep going. It grows dusk, and my clothes are soaked in sweat. I hear a wolf howl in the distance, and then it's joined by more and more howls. I smile and do something I would never have been able to do in New York. I howl as well. I howl and howl and howl with the wolves for what seems like hours, but is really only a few minutes. When I stop, so do the wolves, and all that is left is a beautiful silence. I continue on with a smile on my face, blood pumping in my veins, and a chorus of howls left by the wolves in my heart.

Chapter 22: Timber

I wake up panting heavily with Fern's last words still stuck in my head. I try to calm down and tell myself it was only a dream, but my mind still comes back to the last image and sentence. I shake my head violently and nip myself, yipping a little when I do, to calm myself down. All of the ruckus wakes Opal.

Are you ok Timber? She asks.

I... I will be.

Ok. You can tell me anything. Get it out. I'm right here.

Well, it's just that, have you ever wondered, what would happen if a person you loved just suddenly turned on you and said that they never wanted you anyway? She looks at me, her eyes heavy with sadness and she nuzzles into my fur.

You know that Fern would never do that, right? It was just a nightmare. You can overcome nightmares easily. But what happens in the real world, you can't change unless you change yourself first. And with that she crawls out of the little burrow and onto the grass. I turn over what she said in my mind and shake my head, hoping to clear it, but it just leaves me more confused than before. I eventually push everything out of my mind except for the thought that I could and would never push away, *you need to get to Fern.*

I crawl out after Opal and stretch. I cross over to Opal and stand by her side for a second and sniff the wind for the scent of Fern's car. I catch it in the wind and stand there for a few more seconds holding the smell in my nose, never letting it go. After I come to my senses, I put my nose to the ground and start walking on the path towards Fern. I walk for a little bit before I hear a growl. My head shoots up and I look back at Opal, scared that my nightmare might've come to life, but she just stands there with a funny look on her face. The growling continues and I realize it's just my stomach growling in hunger. As soon as I notice it's my stomach, immediate hunger crawls through my body. I look towards the forest and head in. I come back with a few rats and lay them down on the side of the road for me and Opal to share.

When we finish, I immediately keep going. We walk and walk in silence. In my mind, I hope that we are getting close to Fern, but I can tell that we are as close to Fern as the United States of America is to Asia. A pit of worry forms in my gut as I think of how long it might take to get to her. Three days? Three weeks? A month? A year? Soon, that worry turns to panic as these possibilities argue in my head. I push the argument away as I have done with many thoughts and arguments in my head.

I suddenly notice a boy and his mom and his dog across the street. I watch as the boy picks up his dog and the dog licks his face. The boy laughs and says, "I will never let you go Shade. Never, ever, ever. Because you are the best dog a boy could have!" I stare at them for a bit longer as a pit of tragic sadness forms in my gut, getting bigger by the second. Eventually, Opal nudges me along with her nose and I keep going with her, trailing behind me. As I walk, I try to push away the sadness. I try and try and try, but eventually I give up, because I know that no matter how hard I try, there is some pain that you can't force away.

Chapter 23: Fern

By dawn, I'm burned out and exhausted from walking on crutches for twenty four hours straight. And my armpits and sweaty palms are starting to bleed from the continuous swinging. But I press on. I stop once to go to the bathroom. I set down my make-shift crutches and lower my backpack off of my shoulders and on the ground. I limp over to a tree and hide behind it as I go to the bathroom. My mom used to take me on hikes and long walks, and she taught me how to go to the bathroom outside without being noticed—which, if you think about it, is hard to do in New York. This makes me think about how she taught me everything I know, and how much I miss her. When I finish, I limp back and carefully sit down and pull out the atlas. I open the page to the USA and try to figure out where I am. I track my finger along the states and hold back a groan as I figure out I still have around two hundred seventy nine miles to go. I put the atlas away with some doubt boggling around in my mind.

I sling the backpack onto my shoulders, pick up the crutches, and start again on the path towards Timber. Only after about an hour of swinging, my hands and armpits throb in more pain, and I stop. I take off my backpack and take out my water bottle. I pour a little water into my hands and slosh it around to help with the pain. Then I pour a little water into my shirt on either side right onto my armpits. I breathe a sigh of relief as I do this. After that I put my water bottle away and when I start again, the crutches don't hurt as much.

I keep going until I come upon a blackberry bush. I lick my lips and head a little off the trail and start picking and eating blackberries. When I turn my head to go a little farther to more berries, I see it. A big grizzly bear standing up and staring at me about twenty feet away. I stare back at it and rack my brain quickly for what to do when you encounter a grizzly. I turn my whole body towards it and balance on my good leg and raise my make-shift crutches up above my head and I roar. I don't roar as loud and well as a lion, but I do a pretty loud roar that surprises the grizzly. I don't get any closer and I figure out what to do to get away and stay safe. I keep doing my roar and shaking my make-shift crutches wildly and fiercely above my head while slowly limping backwards away from the grizzly.

I keep going backwards and stop when the grizzly falls back to all four paws and turns his head away from me and starts eating the berries off of the bush, knowing that I'm not a threat. I slowly lower my make-shift crutches under my arms again and head on, keeping my eyes on the bear until I'm far enough away to where I can't see him. Then I go as fast as I can on the way to Timber and slow down only when I'm about five miles away from the bear. I keep going, trying not to think about what would happen if I didn't notice the bear and it got me.

But I'm not afraid of death. Oh no, no, no, no. I'm not afraid of death, I'm afraid of what I would lose if I died. For example, if mom were alive and I was going to die, I would be afraid of never seeing her again, not afraid of death. Like right now, I'm not afraid of dying. In fact, if I died, I might see mom again, but I'm afraid of losing Timber. I'm afraid of not being able to say goodbye.

Chapter 24: Timber

Opal and I keep going throughout the night because I know that the more we travel, the faster we get to Fern. We keep going, but get really tired and sleepy at around midnight, so we look for a place to sleep. Opal barks and I come over to see what she found. An abandoned fox den. I yawn, happy that we found a good resting spot. I head inside first and sniff out the den. It seems safe enough and I bark softly for Opal to come in. But when I bark I hear a growl. I tell Opal to get outside now. She does as told while I go a little deeper into the fox den. Then I realize something. This abandoned fox den has something wrong with it. And what's wrong with it, is that it's not abandoned!

Suddenly a fox leaps out with his jaw stretched wide, ready to catch my skull, but I duck, and all he does is take a bite out of my left ear. I wince in pain, but push through it. I realize how fast and swift the fox is, and doubt looms over me, so I take a chance and try to play a trick. I cower in fear and pain and tell the fox that he's won and I give the den back to him. He places a paw on my body, triumphant. I try not to burst out howling in laughter. After a few seconds, I leap up and chomp down on his right hind leg. He whimpers in pain as I drag him out of the den and throw him into the underbrush with a growl. But as I throw him, he manages to take another bite out of my ear. When he slides into a bush, blood streaming out of his leg, I bark a threat to him and he cowers in response. Opal dashes over to me.

Timber! Are you ok? What happened to your ear?

I'm fine. I guess the den wasn't abandoned, after all. I'm lucky it was just my ear and not somewhere else. But now the den is ours, I played a trick on the fox that I was too scared and in pain to fight, and that he could have the den. Then I laid down in submission, and when he bent over me in triumph, I leapt at his body and chomped down on his leg.

Wow. That's amazing. I'm glad you're smarter than that stupid ol' fox. I'm glad you're okay, Opal says. She licks my nose affectionately and I lick back, then we start into the den, happy that the fox is out. I lay down next to Opal and start licking and cleaning her fur while she rests. I do this until I'm positive she's asleep and I lay my head down on top of hers and fall asleep.

When I wake up, I nudge Opal. She gets up, stretches and heads outside. I follow her and trot out with triumph still washing over myself from last night. I stalk out and come back with a rabbit. Not a lot of food, and we're both really hungry, but it will be enough for a while. We split the rabbit up and eat hastily and greedily. When we finish we lick each other's muzzles clean, and head on.

We go for about an hour when I realize how thirsty I am. I look around and spot a little pond in the distance. I trot over and lap up water until my body is full and tight with water sloshing around inside. After we both get a good drink, we press on. I lift my head high and raise my tail higher than usual, thinking, there's nothing that can stand in our way. But of course, just the opposite happens.

Chapter 25: Timber

We press on for hours, stopping only for a bathroom break. I see a rabbit in a clearing and decide to catch a little snack for a stamina boost. I stalk over quietly and I almost pounce, when I see another wolf staring at me on the other side of the rabbit. I bark to Opal. She trots over and sees the wolf. She growls harshly. I look from her, to the wolf, to the rabbit and do the smartest thing. I pounce on the rabbit and lock its throat between my jaws and hurry back to Opal before the wolf does something to me. But he just stands there looking at us. I decide to be the first to speak, and drop the lifeless rabbit.

Who are you? We don't want trouble. We haven't eaten in days and we need food. That last part was a lie, but I make it sound real by the whine I put in my voice, and Opal soon catches on and as she growls she makes it turn into a fake hacking sound. I suck my breath in so it looks like my ribs are showing from lack of food. The wolf seems pretty convinced and all he does is nod his head, turn away, and walk back from where he came from. I release my breath and smile happily.

It worked! We got the rabbit without any trouble.

Yeah! If you hadn't thought of making us look weak, we never would've made it out alive and well. And with that, we turn back to the path, flop down, and eat the rabbit. When we finish, I get up and sniff the air for the scent of Fern's car. I find it and continue on. Soon I just can't take it any longer and I burst into a run, wanting to find Fern no matter what. Opal runs up beside me and we smile. I lift my head to the sky and howl while we run. I howl with Opal and hear other wolves howl too. Then suddenly, I come to a dead stop and freeze.

What is it Timber?

Hold on a second. I need to check something. And as Opal sits down and cleans her paws, I put my nose to the sky and take in a long breath through my nose. I stare at the sky with elation rising in my body. I look at Opal and she looks at me and I smile and jump up and down on my hind legs howling my happiness and elation. I tell her what I smell and a huge smile creeps onto her face as she jumps up and down howling with me.

115

Because what I smell is the most important thing in the world to smell. Because what I smell is what I've been wanting to smell for so long. Because what I smell is Fern's scent, getting stronger by the second.

Chapter 26: Fern

I reach the end of the forest, and in front of me is a huge field with a hill in the middle. The hill looks so far away, like I would never reach it, but I know with some big effort, I will. I go through the field a little slower because of the amazing smell, feel, and the sound of crickets playing their music. I want to embrace it all.

I start thinking about when I find Timber, what are we going to do? Where are we going to go? I know for sure that we are never ever going back to Dad.

I can't live with my grandparents, that would never work out. I don't have any aunts or uncles, so that won't work either. Wait, couldn't we live, just for a bit, with Jake with either his

117

mom or his dad? No, that wouldn't work out. Would it? No, that could never work out. Could it? I turn it over in my head, feeling even more empty than before. But the more I think about it, the more I feel like it really would work out. I would just stay with his mom or dad until my foot is all healed up, and then I'll find somewhere else to live with just me and Timber and my belongings. Maybe someone will adopt me and love me instead of hating me like Dad. I push him away again and think about this plan for about twenty five minutes. Once I finish the plan it sounds like it would work no matter what.

I'm about fifty feet away from the hill when I see something on top staring at me. At first I think it's a bear, so I get a little closer and see that it's not big enough to be a bear. I get a little closer and realize there's two of them. One of them is a small female wolf that looks a little nervous. But next to her, is not another wolf. Oh no, this is a dog that is banged up and dirty and mucky. This is the same puppy that snuggled with me every night and helped get rid of the pain. It's him!

Chapter 27: Timber

I bark once, then twice, then I'm a huge storm of howling and barking and whining. I howl loudly so that everyone knows what I've found. I've found what I've been searching for all along. I've found Fern!

I bark to her and she whispers my name. Then a huge ear-to-ear grin spreads across her face and she shouts loudly while swinging on sticks. She shouts my name, and I run faster than any dog or wolf has ever run. I run and run and run like a big terrifying monster is going to sweep Fern away for good. But I know one thing. Now that I've found Fern, I'm never letting a big terrifying monster take her away. Because that monster will have to go through me. And he won't want to do that.

Chapter 28: Fern

I hobble towards him as fast as I can on my make-shift crutches. Eventually, I'm so close that I throw my crutches away and run to Timber despite the pain. I run towards him and know that there's nothing that can stop us from reuniting and staying together. Because if someone did, I would go through every fire, every tick, and every bad thing that could happen to me to get to Timber. Because now that he's this close, I'll never let that happen again.

Chapter 29: Timber

I leap on top of her and pin her to the ground and lick her face and wag my tail so much that she has to roll out from underneath me. When she does, she wraps her arms around me so tight, I feel like I will suffocate, but I just smile and keep licking her. Then I remember Opal and I jump away back to Opal. Fern shouts for me to come back, but Opal's important, and she has to come with. I go into the shadows where Opal is and lick her nose.

Come on Opal! Fern is here! She'll love you and you'll love her!

But, but what if she doesn't like me? What if she just throws me out back to the wilderness?

Opal, never say that. She will love you and you will love her. Those are my final words.

You really think so?

No, I don't think so, I know so. After I say that, she looks bolder and follows me out to Fern. Fern holds out her hand and Opal comes and licks it softly. Then Fern laughs, picks up Opal, sets her in her lap, and pets her gently. Opal smiles. I smile and walk over and slump down and cuddle next to Fern. One family. That's what we are. One family united. Nothing will break us again.

Chapter 30: Fern

I pet the female wolf gently in my arms. Her leg has a long jagged scar on it and I pull out the First-Aid kit and find some cream and spread it over the wound. I massage her gently, hoping I'll earn her trust. But I know that as long as Timber loves me, she will too. That's when I notice a huge chunk of Timber's left ear is missing. I cover my mouth with my hand and pat for Timber to come over for treatment. As I spread cream over his ear I use my other hand to rub his stomach.

"Well, it looks like you took risks and got in fights. But I knew you would always be the winner." I hug him tightly, wanting to stop time and just live like this forever. But I know that we have to get to one of Jake's houses sooner than later. And I'd rather not encounter that bear again.

But when I think about it, I feel like if we did encounter that bear and I didn't make it, I wouldn't care. Because my mission was to find Timber and be able to say goodbye before I die, and, mission accomplished. I did what I came to do. Didn't I? But I think about it even more and realize that once you finish a mission, there's actually no finishing. Because life is full of missions and no one as far as I know is able to complete them all. Because you don't just finish a mission, you finish a mission and get prepared for the next one to come. You don't just finish a journey, you finish a journey, and get ready for the next. Because there is never a happily ever after. You don't just get kissed by your prince and assume everything is going to be okay. No, if you think the rest of your life is going to be perfect without a single threat in the world, then you're in a dream that you never wake up from. This is reality; reality is wishing, hoping, and dreaming, and then waking up, and making it all come true.

Chapter 31: Timber

Don't worry Fern, I haven't forgotten. When you said what you did before, I didn't understand it. When you said, "you are mine, I am yours, and we will stay together forever. Nothing can change that," I had no idea it was possible. I thought that death could change that; I thought that what Dad did to me would change that.

But now, I realize we are never really apart. We are always together even though we might not be in the same place. We are two but not two. Oneness. That's what we have. I now know what oneness really is. I knew that we were "two but not two", but I didn't know exactly what "two but not two" was.

But now, I understand. I understand that "two but not two" is two people that will be together no matter what stands in their way. That whoever those two people are, are two halves, and if one of them dies or loses their way, it's like the other person gets their heart split in half and one of them is gone forever. Oneness is getting to each other after something tragic. Oneness is keeping the two halves together. Oneness is the two halves becoming one. Yet, me and Fern were one all along.

The End

About the Author

Seren Kersten is a 5th grader at Geneva Elementary School in Bellingham, Washington. She loves wolves, archery, and everything about the wilderness. She has a little terrier named Max, who is her best friend and always keeps her happy. Their loyalty and love for each other is unbreakable. The theme of this story was inspired by their friendship and how they are "two but not two."